T0380871

Alfonsina and the Ostrich

Story by
Esther Buckley Sutherland

Illustrations by
Georjean Maxwell

Print information available on the last page

Rev. date: 12/18/2018

To order additional copies of this book, contact:
Xlibris
1-888-795-4274
www.Xlibris.com
Orders@Xlibris.com

for Alfonsina and Mara

E.B.S.

special thanks to family and friends
G.M.

Young Alfonsina from Argentina lives on a sprawling ranch with her father Carlos, her mother Nina and her younger brother, little Carlos. They have a hunting dog named Mara.

On the far side of their ranch house sits an old gnarled tree. Alfonsina calls it her thinking tree. Whenever she and little Carlos quarrel, she clambers up the tree to her favorite branch and lets her thoughts wander until she is ready to come down.

She Know this is her safe spot because Carlos is too little to climb trees.

One sunny morning the children had a HUMONGOUS quarrel. Alfonsina became so angry and unhappy that she decided to run away from home. She followed the dirt road to a big gate, opened it, and marched toward the tall pampas grasses and the open fields beyond. It was springtime, but Alfonsina was too upset to notice the green grasses besprinkled with colorful flowers. Her dog went with her.

Mara ran ahead flushing squawking birds from their hiding places. She snorted and sniffed for armadillos and hares, and soon was out of sight.

Staying on the winding path along the hedgerows and tall grasses, Alfonsina soon came to a curve in the road.

As she rounded the bend, she suddenly found herself face to face with a monstrous black cow.

Alfonsina stood still, petrified! Even though she was used to seeing hundreds of their cows roaming the pastures, Alfonsina had never been THIS CLOSE to one such creature. She was TOO close for comfort.

The cow, with her curious BIG brown eyes, stared at Alfonsina with a steady wide-eyed gaze as if to say... "Where did you come from, and what are you doing standing on my pathway?"

Ever so slowly... Alfonsina started to walk backwards. The cow, chewing her cud and swishing her tail back and forth, turned and sauntered away from Alfonsina. "Whew," muttered Alfonsina with a sigh of relief. "I almost bumped into her! I wonder whom Dad was talking about when he warned us about mean critters or a Mr. Longlegs. She saw Mara appear briefly... then scurry back into the long grasses.

Alfonsina stayed on the well-trodden path toward the hills. Much later and feeling a little weary, Alfonsina came to a fence. Her eyes followed the fence to a big gate. She ran and climbed up on the gate to rest, and watch the ranch horses graze near the lake. After awhile, she jumped down and continued walking. "Where is Mara?" she wondered, "She's been gone such a long time."

Suddenly she heard a horrendous noise...

There it was again, a thunderous ROAR... then frantic yowling and squealing. Alfonsina looked up and saw Mara racing down the hill, yelping, and fleeing faster than a hare, her paws barely touching the ground. NO WONDER!! Behind the frightened dog was a GIGANTIC OSTRICH with long powerful legs running at a furious speed through the grasses and onto the path. Like a warrior in full dress, toes pounding, shaking the earth, it was trying to kick Mara.

THE OSTRICH WAS WILD WITH RAGE!

They were heading straight toward Alfonsina!

She froze in terror.

16

THEN SUDDENLY...
MARA SAW ALFONSINA!

The plucky dog did an abrupt
roundabout... into the long grasses
away from Alfonsina with the ostrich
following. The huge fierce angry
bird and the howling dog disappeared
from sight.

Trembling with fright, Alfonsina turned, bound for home, hurrying as fast as she could. When she reached the fence, she scrambled onto the highest post, and looked around. In the distance, she could see the ostrich speeding through the grasslands, chasing Mara. Then they disappeared over the horizon.

Alfonsina sped home, wailing and worrying about Mara. As she approached the ranch, she could hear heavy panting behind her. When she turned around, she saw Mara.

"Oh, Mara, it's you!" she sobbed, hugging her beloved dog.

"Let's go home, Girl!" Mara stayed close to Alfonsina who noticed a slight cut on her back.

23

When little Carlos saw Alfonsina, he ran to greet her.

"Alfonsina, where have you been?" he said, "Mom and Dad have been looking all over for you!"

"I went for a walk," Alfonsina said quietly.

"I'm sorry I was mean to you this morning, Alfonsina. I won't be mean to you again, I promise," her little brother said as he grabbed her hand. Alfonsina squeezed his hand affectionately. She was so glad to be home.

"Oh, there you are, Alfonsina," called Mom. "Come and have breakfast, you must be hungry!" Alfonsina was famished. She gave Mara fresh water and tended to the cut on the dog's back before sitting down to eat. Mara stayed by Alfonsina's feet. She knew she would get some of Alfonsina's breakfast as well as her own.

That afternoon, the family had tea and cake on the front porch. Their view stretched beyond the ranch fence and cattle path to a large lake where the animals go to drink.

"Look!" yelled little Carlos. He pointed to a HUGE ostrich proudly trotting with its SEVEN CHICKS toward the water.

"That's Mr. Longlegs," exclaimed Alfonsina, looking over at Mara, and thinking about the terrifying adventure they had shared.

Mara was watching the ostrich but she did not move.

She had had quite enough of that big bird!

The end.

Printed in the United States
By Bookmasters